Music Theory Workbook for Guitar

Volume One
Chord and Interval
Construction

by
Bruce Arnold

Muse Eek Publishing Company
New York, New York

ISBN 0-9648632-4-3

Printed in the United States

This publication can be purchased from your local bookstore or by contacting:
Muse Eek Publishing Company
P.O. Box 509
New York, NY 10276, USA
Phone: 212-473-7030
Fax: 212-473-4601
http://www.muse-eek.com
sales@muse-eek.com

Table Of Contents

Acknowledgments

The author would like to thank Michal Shapiro for her patience and help in proof reading and helpful suggestions. A very special thank you to Tina Sobin for her editing and proof reading which saved the author many many hours of work.

About the Author

Bruce Arnold is from Sioux Falls, South Dakota. His educational background started with 3 years of music study at the University of South Dakota; he then attended the Berklee College of Music where he received a Bachelor of Music degree in composition. During that time he also studied privately with Jerry Bergonzi and Charlie Banacos.

Mr. Arnold has taught at some of the most prestigious music schools in America, including the New England Conservatory of Music, Dartmouth College, Berklee College of Music, Princeton University and New York University. He is a performer, composer, jazz clinician and has an extensive private instruction practice.

Currently Mr. Arnold is performing with his own "The Bruce Arnold Trio," and "Eye Contact" with Harvie Swartz, as well as with two experimental bands, "Release the Hounds" a free improv group, and "Spooky Actions" which re-interprets the work of 20th Century classical masters.

His debut CD "Blue Eleven" (MMC 2036J) received great critical acclaim, and his most recent CD "A Few Dozen" was released in January 2000. The Los Angeles Times said of this release "Mr. Arnold deserves credit for his effort to expand the jazz palette."

For more information about Mr. Arnold check his website at http://www.arnoldjazz.com This website contains audio examples of Mr. Arnold's compositions and a workshop section with free downloadable music exercises.

Foreword

Many of my students have asked me how they can improve their music theory and fretboard knowledge. This book is an attempt to fill those needs.

Learning the language of music is imperative to becoming a professional musician or communicating intelligently with other musicians, but more importantly, applying this knowledge to your instrument will give you the ability to create music with greater flexibility , coherence, and confidence.

Future volumes of this Music Theory Workbook series will cover scales and diatonic chords of a key both of which are very important to playing and understanding music. See the final pages of this book for a complete listing and description of current music related publications.

Muse Eek Publishing has created a website with a FAQ forum for all my books. If you have any questions about anything contained in this book feel free to contact me at FAQ@muse-eek.com and I will happy to post an answer to your question. My goal is to educate and help you reach a higher degree of musical ability.

A very special thank you goes to Tina Sobin for her patient and meticulous work in editing this book.

Bruce Arnold
New York, New York

Theory Workbook for Guitar Volume One

   This theory workbook is designed to teach you the basic building blocks of music theory and how to apply these to the guitar fretboard. Each exercise presents a group of intervals or chords which must be written using staff notation and guitar chord diagrams. This method will instill the information in your head and your hands. Direct physical application of music theory makes it more relevant and greatly helps in learning the guitar fretboard.

   Background theory information needed to complete each exercise is presented in easy to understand language. This is followed by exercises for learning intervals and triads, 7th chords (4 note chords) and chords with tensions. The answers are in the back of the book.

   The exercises are designed for a 24 fret guitar so keep this in mind when completing the chord diagrams. The notes contained in each chord will fit into the chord diagram supplied with each exercise. Make sure to fit your answer into this diagram. You can place more than one note on each string. The answers are not meant to be played as a chord but as an arpeggio (one note after another).

   For each exercise in this book you will need to find the intervals or chord tones/tensions. Each example will require you to figure out where the notes would be on a staff and where these notes would be located on a guitar. Remember that memorizing the notes contained in each chord presented combined with knowing where these notes are on the guitar will open up a whole new understanding of music. Here's how each example will appear:

A full explanation of the chord diagrams can be found on page 14.

   Study the theory section that follows. If you wish to work on the pertinent exercises, you will find the pages on which these exercises appear given along with the theory presented. Try applying each completed exercise to songs or chord vamps you know, so that your ear can get comfortable with each new sound.

Music theory and chord construction

The first thing a student must tackle is learning how to read music. A detailed description of the development of music notation is beyond the scope of this book and some inconsistencies (which will appear in italics) have stayed in musical notation, in the course of that development. For the beginner these inconsistencies can be very confusing but inconsistent as it may be, music notation does have a standard for expressing itself visually and by understanding this system the world of western music is open to you.

In this system a series of lines and spaces are employed to create a visual representation of sound. Each line and space corresponds to a pitch. Each pitch is given a name A, B, C, D, E, F, or G. A clef sign is also used to designate what names each line and space will receive. The reason for the many types of clefs will be explained momentarily. First let us look at the treble clef. The treble clef places the note sequence in the order listed below. This complete system of lines and spaces with a clef sign is called a staff.

As can be seen in the examples each line and space corresponds to a different tone. If you want to have pitches higher or lower than the 5 lines and four spaces you can extend the staff by using ledger lines. Ledger lines give you the ability to represent higher and lower pitches by extending the staff, these extended pitches are called ledger line notes.

If we extend this idea we run into trouble as can be seen from the example below. When excessive ledger lines are used, reading music becomes very difficult. To alleviate this problem other clefs are employed to make reading these notes that are out of the treble clef's range easier. The note in the previous example would be found in the bass or F clef on the 2nd space.

C note

The same C in bass clef

The following example shows where the notes fall in the bass clef. We will only use the treble clef in this book but a basic understanding of the bass clef is important.

2

If we look at our treble clef again we notice that there is an "e" on the first line and a "e" on the 4th space. Our ear recognizes these pitches as being the same pitch but the "e" on the 4th space sounds like a higher version of the low "e". In musical terminology the higher "e" is said to sound an octave higher than the lower "e". If we play these two "e's" on the guitar it would be the 2nd fret on the D string and fifth fret on the B string.

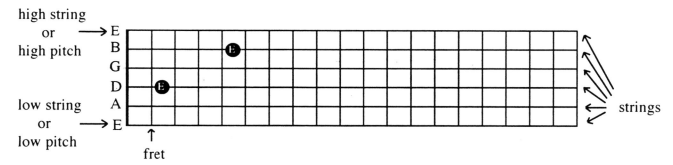

To summarize what we have learned so far: there are 7 pitches which are represented on a staff with the letter names A,B,C,D,E,F,G. These 7 pitches keep repeating themselves in different octaves. To represent these notes in other octaves we need to use ledger lines or other clefs.

One of the inconsistencies of the notation system we have learned so far is that it doesn't show all the available notes in western music. There are a total of 12 pitches used in western music which of course as we have learned can be found in many different octaves. To show all 12 notes in the system, "sharp"(#) and "flat" (b) symbols are used to represent the tones that occur between the letter names of the notes. For example between the note C and D there exists a pitch which can be called either C sharp or D flat. These notes are represented as follows: C# or Db. The (#) and (b) symbols work in the following way, the flat (b) lowers a pitch and a sharp (#) which raises the pitch. If a note is sharped it is said to have been raised a half step; if it is flatted it is said to have been lowered a half step. **A half step is the smallest distance possible in western music.** If we show all 12 notes on the staff within one octave we get what is called the chromatic scale. This scale contains all possible notes in the western system of music. Notice that there is no sharp or flat between E and F and B and C which is just one of those inconsistencies you have to accept with this notational system. Both chromatic scales shown below sound the same on the guitar; the decision to use sharps or flats depends on the musical situation. You will notice that the D in the chromatic scale with flats has a symbol in front of it. This symbol is called a natural sign. It is used to cancel the flat that appears before the previous D. **In written music, measures are used to delineate time, and sharps and flats carry through the whole measure until a new measure starts, unless a natural symbol is used to cancel it.**

Chromatic Scale

3

The 12 note chromatic scale can be represented in either of the two examples listed above. Remember a C# is the same note as a Db on the guitar. If you play on only one string of the guitar and move consecutively up each fret you will be playing a chromatic scale. If you were to play the above two examples of a chromatic scale you would start on the A string 3rd fret and move up each fret until you reach the 15th fret to complete the chromatic scale.

Guitar Fretboard

Though the chromatic scale represents all 12 notes, much of western music of the last few centuries has been based around only 7 tones. If we extract these 7 notes as shown below we end up with a major scale.

Major scale derived from Chromatic scale

If we look at the distance in half steps between the notes of a major scale we see a pattern; whole, whole, half, whole, whole, whole, half. **All major scales are based on these intervals.**

C Major Scale

4

If we apply this to the guitar fretboard the information works out accordingly: start on any note on the guitar and move up on one string starting with a whole step (2 frets), whole step, half step (1 fret), whole step, whole step, whole step, half step. This is one way to play a major scale on the guitar.

Guitar Fretboard

With this information you could play any major scale by following the pattern of whole step, whole step, half step, whole step, whole step, whole step, half step. The example below shows a D major scale.

Guitar Fretboard

The notes of a C major scale C, D, E, F, G, A, B are commonly referred to as the diatonic notes of the key of C major. If we had the key of D major the diatonic notes would be D, E, F#, G, A, B, C#

If we use the major scale formula (1,1,1/2,1,1,1,1/2) we can figure out every major scale. We will find that each key has a different number of sharps or flats. If a piece of music uses a particular key, its key signature is placed at the beginning of the piece of music. The following is a list of all the sharps and flats found in various keys. These are commonly referred to as the key signatures, and they occur after the clef sign and at the beginning of each line of music. "Music Theory Workbook for Guitar Volume Two" will cover learning all scales and their associated keys.

Whole steps and half steps are the basic building blocks for the major scale. The whole step equals two half steps. The distance between two notes is called an interval. For example the distance between C and D is a whole step. This is also called a major second interval. It is important to know intervals because chords are frequently named for the intervals in their internal structure. All two note interval combinations from the root of the major scale are listed below.

| Major 2nd | Major 3rd | *Perfect 4th* | *Perfect 5th* |
| 2 half steps | 4 half steps | 5 half steps | 7 half steps |

| Major 6th | Major 7th | Octave |
| 9 half steps | 11 half steps | 12 half steps |

If we sharp any of these intervals we create an augmented interval. If we flat a major second, third, sixth, or seventh, we create a minor interval. If we flat a perfect fourth, a fifth, or an octave, we get a diminished interval, and *if we double flat the major 7th we have a diminished 7th*. The following is a list of some of the more common augmented, minor and diminished intervals. These are explored in all keys with the "Basic Intervals" exercise on page 16.

| augmented unison | minor 2nd | augmented 2nd | minor 3rd |
| 1 half steps | 1 half steps | 3 half steps | 3 half steps |

| augmented 4th or tritone | diminished 5th or flat 5 | augmented 5th | minor 6th |
| 6 half steps | 6 half steps | 8 half steps | 8 half steps |

| diminished 7th | augmented 6th | minor 7th |
| 9 half steps | 10 half steps | 10 half steps |

If we continue past the octave, intervals are given new names to show that they are more than an octave apart. The larger intervals exercise on page 17 covers these intervals. Here are a few examples.

An augmented interval may be written in different ways. A (+) may appear before the number, or a (#) or (aug). If the interval is flatted it is usually indicated with a flat. Here are some of the common interval names you will need to know.

This knowledge of the chromatic scale, major scale and the construction of intervals are crucial tools to understanding the internal structure of chords.

So far we have discussed 2 note intervals, sometimes called diads. When we add one more note to our 2 note interval we create a chord. A chord can be a combination of any 3 or more notes played at the same time. Western music can build chords using a wide variety of intervals. One of the most common ways to build chords is to stack up diatonic 3rd intervals. For example if we took C in the key of C and stacked up 3rds we would get C, E, and G because all of those notes are in the key of C and are a 3rd apart. **These structures built in thirds are commonly referred to as triads and the C note is said to be the root of the chord.**

C Major Triad

If we continue this process and build up diatonic triads above all the notes of C major we get the following 3 note structures.

Triads derived from stacking 3rds above a C major scale

These seven chords structures have a certain internal structure. The first structure C, E, and G form what is called a major chord, if we measure the distance or interval between each note using our chromatic scale we can find the formula for building major chords. Between C and E is 4 half steps or a major third. Between E and G is 3 half steps or a minor third. Therefore to create a major chord we need to combine a major third on the bottom and a minor third on the top. You will notice that the chord starting on F and on G are also major chords. The exercise on page 18 will cover major triads.

C major chord

minor 3rd
3 half steps

major 3rd
4 half steps

The second structure D, F, and A form what is called a minor chord. Using the chromatic scale once again we can find the formula for building minor chords. Between D and F is 3 half steps or a minor third. Between F and A is 4 half steps or a major third. Therefore to create a minor chord we need to combine a minor third on the bottom and a major third on the top. You will notice that the chord starting on E and on A are also minor chords. The exercise on page 19 will cover minor triads.

D minor chord

major 3rd
4 half steps

minor 3rd
3 half steps

8

This leaves us with one last structure B, D, F which forms what is called a diminished chord. Using the same method we find that the distance between B and D is 3 half steps or a minor third. Between D and F is 3 half steps or a minor third. Therefore to create a diminished chord we need to combine a minor third on the bottom and a minor third on the top. The exercise on page 20 will cover diminished triads.

B diminished chord

minor 3rd
3 half steps

minor 3rd
3 half steps

Below is a list of all the triads and their chord names. These chords are referred to as the diatonic triad or chords of a major key. You will see each of these chords labeled in many ways. C major could be shown as: C major, CMaj, C, CM, D minor could be shown as: D minor, Dmin, D-, Dm, B diminished could be shown as: B diminished, B dim, or B°.

They are also numbered sequentially which allows someone to refer to the D minor chord in the key of C, as a "II chord". Because many contemporary tunes are written using only the diatonic chords of a key it is a very common practice among musicians to learn the diatonic chords of every key using numbers and letters to aid in the memorization and quick learning of new songs. "Music Theory Workbook for Guitar Volume Three" will cover learning these Diatonic Chords in all keys.

Diatonic chords of C Major

C	D-	E-	F	G	A-	B°
I	II	III	IV	V	VI	VII

9

If we take the three types of chords learned so far and write them out with C as the root we come up with (ex. 1) C, E, G for a C major chord which is a major third stacked below a minor third, (ex. 2) C, Eb, G for a C minor chord which has just the opposite interval combination; a minor third stacked below a major third, and (ex. 3) C, Eb, Gb for a diminished chord which is two minor third intervals. You may notice that we have not yet discussed the combination of a major third and major third which is shown in (ex. 4) C, E, G#. This combination is called an augmented chord and is written as follows: C augmented, C aug, C+. The augmented chord can be found as a diatonic chord in other scales which are discussed in the "Music Theory Workbook for Guitar Volume Two." The exercise on page 21 will cover augmented chords.

There are two more triad chord structures that are commonly found in contemporary music; the suspended 4th chord (sus 4) and the add 9th (add 9). The sus 4 is a triad in which the 4th has replaced the 3rd. This creates an unusual structure of 5 half steps or a 4th and 2 half steps or a major 2nd. The suspended chord can be a diatonic chord built on the 1st, 2nd, 3rd, 5th, or 6th degrees. It is common to see the suspended chord written as C4, C sus or C sus4. The add 9 replaces the 3rd with the second. The interval structure of this chord would be 2 half steps or a major 2nd and 5 half steps or a perfect 4th. The add 9 chord can be a diatonic chord build on the 1st, 2nd, 4th 5th or 6th degrees of the scale. The exercise on page 21 covers sus 4 and page 45 add 9 triads.

The notes of each chord are called the chord tones. For example, the chord tones of a C major chord are C, E, and G. It is also possible to build chords that contain more notes. The next most common chord type is a four note structure which is commonly referred to as a 7th chord. To build a 7th chord you add a note a third above the triads we have just discussed. If we add a major third above our C major triad we get C, E, G B

If we go back to our diatonic triads of C major and add a diatonic third above each chord we now have the diatonic 7th chords of the key of C major.

7th Chords derived from C major scale

These seven 7th chords structures have a certain internal structure just as our triads did. The first structure (C, E, G and B) contains the triad C, E and G plus another major third up to B. This structure is called a major 7th chord. If we again measure the distance or interval between each note using our chromatic scale we can find the formula for building major 7th chords. Between C and E is 4 half steps or a major third, between E and G is 3 half steps or a minor third, G to B is 4 half steps or a major third. **Therefore to create a major 7th chord we need to combine a major third on the bottom and a minor third in the middle and a major third on the top.** You will notice that the chord starting on F is also a major 7th chord. The exercise on page 24 will cover major 7th chords.

C major 7th chord

The second structure (D, F, A and C), forms what is called a minor 7th chord. Using the chromatic scale once again, we can find the formula for building minor 7th chords. Between D and F is 3 half steps or a minor third. Between F and A is 4 half steps or a major third; between A and C is 3 half steps or a minor third. **Therefore to create a minor 7th chord we need to combine a minor third on the bottom and a major third in the middle and a minor third on the top.** You will notice that the chord starting on E and on A are also minor 7th chords. The exercise on page 25 will cover minor 7th chords.

D minor 7th chord

11

The third new structure G, B, D and F forms a dominant 7th chord. Using the chromatic scale we can find the formula for building dominant 7th chords. Between G and B is 4 half steps or a major third, between B and D is 3 half steps or a minor third, between D and F is 3 half steps or a minor third. **Therefore to create a dominant 7th chord we need to combine a major third on the bottom and a minor third in the middle and a minor third on the top.** Only one dominant seventh chord can appear naturally within any major key. The exercise on page 26 will cover dominant 7th chords.

G dominant 7th chord

The last structure B, D, F and A form what is called a minor 7 flat 5, also referred to as the "half diminished" chord. Using the chromatic scale we can find the formula for building minor 7 flat 5 chords. Between B and D is 3 half steps or a minor third, between D and F is 3 half steps or a minor third and between F and A is 4 half steps or a major third. **Therefore to create a minor 7b5 chord we need to combine a minor third on the bottom and a minor third in the middle and a major third on the top.** The minor 7b5, like the dominant 7th, happens only once in diatonic 7th chords of a major key. The exercise on page 28 will cover minor 7b5 chords.

B minor 7 flat 5 chord

The 7th chords can be organized in the same manner as our triads were. Below is a list of the diatonic 7th chords of a major key. These chords again can be labeled in many ways: C major 7 could be shown as C major 7, CMaj7, CΔ7, CM7. D minor 7 could be shown as D minor 7, Dmin 7, D-7, Dm7. G dominant 7th could be shown as G dominant, G dom7, or G7. B minor 7th flat 5 can be shown as B minor 7b5, Bmin7b5, and B-7b5.

The same numbering system applies for the 7th chords as for the triads.

Here are the chords listed sequentially with their chord names and degrees.

Diatonic 7th chords of C Major

Most styles of music generally use triads or 7th chords with or without tensions. For instance, folk music gravitates toward triads while jazz tends to use more 7th chords and even more complicated structures.

If we extend the idea of adding more notes to chords by extending up another 3rd above our 7th tone we create 9th chords. Therefore CΔ7 (C, E, G, B) becomes CΔ79 (C, E, G, B, D), the interval formula would be maj3, min3, maj3, min3. The 9th is a tension, not a chord tone. A tension in contemporary music is a non chord tone which adds color to our basic triads and 7th chords.

The method of using intervals by calculating half steps gets very time consuming as the chord structures get larger and larger. **There is a faster way to calculate which notes are contained in any chord but this requires that you first memorize the major scale.** If we go back and look at our C major scale we can see that to find for example, a major 7 chord which is C, E, G, and B we need only to think the 1, 3, 5, 7 degrees of the C major scale. To add on a tension like the 9th we simply add the 2nd degree of the C major scale which is a D. When the 2nd is placed above the 7th it is called the 9th. We need only to add the 2nd degree of C (which we have learned is the same note as the 9th). The exercises on starting on page 38 will cover chords with tensions.

Δ9th chord

If we use the major scale as our reference point in figuring out chord tones we only need to know the formula for each chord type. For example: a C-7 chord would be C, Eb, G, Bb which would be 1, b3, 5 and b7 in the key of C. Therefore by memorizing the structure of each chord and altering the notes from the major scale we can quickly find the correct notes for any chord. Below is a list of the triads and seventh chords found in this book and their relationship to a C major scale.

triad chords (exercises found on page 18 to 22)
major	(1 3 5)
minor	(1 b3 5)
diminished	(1 b3 b5)
augmented	(1 3 #5)
sus4	(1,4,5)

7th chords (exercises found on page 24 to 36)
Δ7	(1 3 5 7)
-7	(1 b3 5 b7)
7	(1 3 5 b7)
-7b5	(1 b3 b5 b7)
°7	(1 b3 b5 bb7)
-Δ7	(1 b3 5 7)
7sus4	(1 4 5 b7)
Δ7#5	(1 3 #5 7)
7#5	(1 3 #5 b7)
Δ7#11	(1 3 #4 7)
7#11	(1 3 #4 b7)
6	(1 3 5 6)

When we add even more tensions to our triads or seventh chords we simply have to add the appropriate note from our reference major scale. For example: Cdom9 would be C, E, G, Bb, D or 1, 3, 5, b7, and 9th degrees of a C major scale. Tensions are applied in the exercises starting on page 38.

C reference scale

flat the (B) for b7

As each chord type is presented in this book a review is made of the available tensions for each chord type. A brief overview of how each chord type is used is also included.

The chord diagrams used in this book are explained below. When completing the exercises you do not have to put the name of the notes within each black circle.

chord diagrams

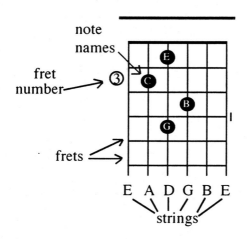

It must be mentioned that the guitar is a transposing instrument sounding an octave (12 half steps) lower than written. Therefore middle C on a piano appears as the C one ledger line below the staff while the actual sound of middle C on the guitar is 1st fret on the B string. All staff notation in this book is transposed.

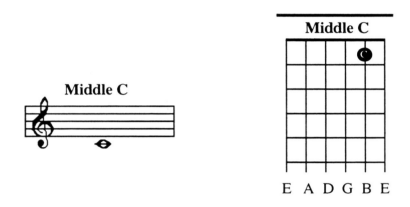

Therefore the open strings on the guitar would be written as follows:

Basic Intervals

Larger Intervals

Major Triads

18

Minor Triads

Diminished Triads

Augmented Triads

Suspended 4th Triads

Seventh Chords

Pages 24 to 36 will present exercises covering seventh chords. A complete list of the 7th chords is found below. Make sure you understand each chord type before proceeding to the exercises. If you need to review 7th chords and their construction they can be found on page 11 and 12.

There are 13 basic Seventh chord types:

Δ7	1,3,5,7
-7	1,b3,5,b7
7	1,3,5,b7
7sus4	1,4,5,b7
-7b5	1,b3,b5,b7
°7	1,b3,b5,bb7
-Δ7	1,b3,5,7
Δ7#11	1,3,#4,7
Δ7#5	1,3,#5,7
7b5	1,3,b5,b7
7#5	1,3,#5,b7
6th	1,3,5,6
-6	1,b3,5,6

It is a very good idea to memorize the structures of these chords. I find that relating them all back to the major seventh is a good idea. Therefore a -Δ7 is a major seventh with a flatted 3..

Major Seventh Chords

Minor Seventh Chords

Dominant Seventh Chords

Dominant Seventh Sus4 Chords

Minor 7b5 Chords

Diminished 7th Chords

Minor Major Seventh Chords

Major 7#11 Chords

Major 7#5 Chords

Example

Dominant Seventh b5 Chords

33

Dominant Seventh #5 Chords

Major 6th Chords

Minor 6th Chords

Chord Tones and Tensions
Major 7th
Δ7
Chord Tones 1 3 5 7
Tensions 9 #11 13

Chords with Tensions

As has been previously discussed "tensions" can be added to chords to give them more "color". Before each chord type is shown, the possible tensions for that chord will be given. The chord tones and tensions for CΔ7 are as follows:

All the tensions that we learn for each chord can be used as a substitute for the basic chord type. For instance if we have a C chord we could substitute CΔ7 or CΔ79 etc. Theoretically this will work but you must use your ear to decide whether the sound is appropriate for the chords before and after it, and for the style of music you are playing.

Major 7 9 Chords

Major 7 6 Chords

Major 7 6 #11 Chords

Major 7 9 #11 Chords

Major 7 6 9 Chords

Example

Major 6 9 Chords

Major 7 6 9 #11 Chords

Major add 9 Chords

Major 7 6 9 #11 Chords

46

Chord Tones and Tensions
Minor 7th
-7
Chord Tones 1 b3 5 b7
Tensions 9 11 13

Chords with Tensions

Below is a list of the chord tones and tensions for a minor 7th chord. When used in a jazz context it is common to add tensions to the -7 to give it more "color". When used in a jazz tune the minor 7th chords can sound fine if it is used without tensions. This is especially true when it is the II chord of a II V I progression; however if a minor 7th is the I minor, a minor chord that is part of a vamp, or is in a ballad it is more common to add tensions.

The chord tones and tensions for C-7 are as follows:

Be careful when adding tensions to a minor chord especially when adding the 9th. Sometimes the 9th can conflict, especially when the minor chord is build on the 3rd degree of a key. As always you must use your ear to decide whether the added tension is appropriate and if it sounds good with the chords before and after it. Different styles will again affect which tensions sound the best.

Minor 9th Chords

Minor 9 11 Chords

Minor 6 9 Chords

Minor 6 9 11 Chords

Minor 11 Chords

Minor 6 7 Chords

Minor 7 6 9 Chords

Chord Tones and Tensions
Dominant 7th
7
Chord Tones 1 3 5 b7
Tensions b9 9 #9 #11 #5 13

Chords with Tensions

Below is a list of the chord tones and tensions for a dominant chord. Once again there is no limit to how many tensions can be in a chord, but because the guitar has only 6 strings we are limited to 6 notes.

The chord tones and tensions for C7 are as follows:

All the tensions that we learn for each chord can be used as a substitute for the basic chord type. Dominant chords have many possibilities for adding and combining tensions. For instance if we have a C7 chord we could substitute C7#11 or C7#9b13 etc. Theoretically any combination is possible. Usually tensions are not combined that are a half step apart. For example, you usually don't have a dominant chord which contains "b9" and natural 9. Also most of these half step possibilities make for difficult and awkward playing on the guitar.

Although any tension combination is possible there are common situations where certain tensions are preferred over others. When a dominant chord resolves up a fourth to a major chord i.e. C7 to FΔ7 it is common to use natural tensions 9 or 13. When a dominant chord resolves up a fourth to a minor chord i.e. C7 to F-7 it is common to use the altered tensions b9, #9, #11, b13. The reason C7 to FΔ7 uses natural tension is that the 9 and 13 (in this case, on C7 that would be D and A), are diatonic to the F major scale therefore creating an expectation of an impending major resolution. On the other hand if C7 resolves to an F minor chord, the altered tensions (in this case, on C7 they would be Db, Eb, Ab) are commonly used because they are found in various F minor scales. Db and Ab could be from the F harmonic minor scale and Eb from the natural minor scale. There are of course many other F minor scales that these three notes are found in. You can find many examples of these different tension combinations in the progression section found at the end of "Chord Workbook for Guitar Volume One."

Dominant 9th Chords

Dominant 7b9 Chords

Dominant 7#9 Chords

Dominant 13 Chords

Dominant 7b13 Chords

61

Dominant 9 13 Chords

Dominant 9 b13 Chords

Dominant 7 b9 13 Chords

Dominant 7 #9 13 Chords

65

Dominant 7 b9 b13 Chords

Dominant 7 #9 b13 Chords

Dominant 9 #11 Chords

Dominant 7 b9 #11 Chords

Dominant 7 #9 #11 Chords

Dominant 7 #11 13 Chords

Dominant 7 #11 b13 Chords

Chord Tones and Tensions
Dominant 7th sus4
7sus4
Chord Tones 1 4 5 b7
Tensions b9 9 #9 10 b13 13

Chords with Tensions

Below is a list of the chord tones and tensions for a dominant 7th sus4 chord. Dominant 7th sus4 is commonly found in jazz where there is vamp or also it is placed before a dominant 7th. For example C7sus4 to C7. Like the minor 7th chord the 7sus4 chord can sound fine if it is used without tensions.

The chord tones and tensions for C7sus4 are as follows:

Many of the voicings of the dominant 7sus4 chords on guitar contain a lot of 4th intervals. This creates a very "open" sound and is commonly used for vamps. It is also common to use the 7sus4 voicing as a vehicle to slide in and out of a key center by moving the chord up and down a half step or to other intervals. An example of this application can be found in the E minor blues progression on page 117 of the Chord Workbook for Guitar Volume 1.

Dominant 9sus4 Chords

Dominant 7sus4b9 Chords

Dominant 7sus4#9 Chords

Dominant 13sus4 Chords

Dominant 7sus4b13 Chords

Dominant 9sus4 13 Chords

Dominant 9sus4 b13 Chords

80

Dominant 7sus4 b9 13 Chords

Dominant 7sus4 #9 13 Chords

Dominant 7sus4 b9 b13 Chords

Dominant 7sus4 #9 b13 Chords

Dominant 13sus4 add10 Chords

Chord Tones and Tensions
Minor 7th flat 5
-7b5
Chord Tones 1 b3 b5 b7
Tensions 9 11 b13

Chords with Tensions

Below is a list of the chord tones and tensions for a minor 7b5 chord. Minor 7b5 is commonly found in jazz as a II chord in a II V I of minor. For example D-7b5 to G7b9 to C-7 Like the minor 7th chord the -7b5 chord can sound fine if it is used without tensions. Because of the fingering difficulty associated with adding tensions to a -7b5 chord guitarists frequently don't add in tensions when playing this chord. The tensions do create a great sound when the situation allows, so don't be afraid to experiment.

The chord tones and tensions for -7b5 are as follows:

Minor 7b5 add 9 Chords

Minor 7b5 add b13 Chords

Chord Tones and Tensions
Diminished 7th
°7
Chord Tones 1 b3 b5 bb7
Tensions 9 11 b13 b15

Chords with Tensions

Below is a list of the chord tones and tensions for a diminished 7th chord. °7 is commonly found in jazz as a passing chord. For example CΔ7 to C#°7 to D-7. you will also find the °7 as a I diminished chord. For example: CΔ7 to C°7 to CΔ7. Like the minor 7th chord the °7 chord can sound fine if it is used without tensions. Because of the fingering difficulty associated with adding tensions to a °7 chord guitarist frequently don't add in tensions when playing this chord. Tensions do create a great sound when the situation allows, so don't be afraid to experiment.

The chord tones and tensions for °7 are as follows:

Diminished 7th add 9 Chords

Diminished 7th add 11 Chords

Diminished 7th add b13 Chords

Diminished 7th add Major 7th Chords

Chord Tones and Tensions
Minor Major 7th
-Δ7
Chord Tones 1 b3 5 7
Tensions 9 11 #11 13

Chords with Tensions

Below is a list of the chord tones and tensions for a -Δ7 chord. -Δ7 is commonly used in jazz as a substitute chord for a minor 7th. For example rather than D-7b5 to G7b9 to C-7 you would use D-7b5 to G7b9 to C-Δ7. When a -7 chord is the last chord of a song the -Δ7 is a commonly used as a replacement. This creates a sound that really feels like the song has ended . For example if the song ends on a C-7 you could replace it with a C-Δ7. Like the minor 7th chord the -Δ7 chord can sound fine if it is used without tensions. Again, because of the fingering difficulty associated with adding tensions to a -Δ7 chord guitarist frequently don't add in tensions when playing this chord. By the way, I highly recommend using the -Δ7b5 chord as an ending chord, it sounds great.

The chord tones and tensions for -Δ7 are as follows:

Minor Major 7 9 Chords

Minor Major 7 11 Chords

Minor Major 7 6 Chords

Minor Major 7 9 11 Chords

Minor Major 7 6 9 Chords

Minor Major 7 6 11 Chords

Minor Major 7b5 Chords

Minor Major 7b5 add9 Chords

Minor Major 7b5 add11 Chords

Chord Tones and Tensions
Major 7th sharp 5
Δ7#5
Chord Tones 1 3 #5 7
Tensions 9 #11

Chords with Tensions

Below is a list of the chord tones and tensions for a Δ7#5 chord. Δ7#5 is commonly used in jazz as a substitute chord for a Δ7 chord. For example rather than D-7 to G7 to CΔ7 you would use D-7 to G7 to CΔ7#5. When a Δ7 chord is the last chord of a song the Δ7#5 is a commonly used as a replacement. This creates a highly colorful sound that really spices up the end of a tune . For example if the song ends on a CΔ7 you could replace it with a CΔ7#5. Like the minor 7th chord the CΔ7#5 chord can sound fine if it is used without tensions. This is another example of infrequently added tensions due to fingering difficulties. But if you can do it, the rewards are there. I highly recommend using the CΔ7#5 chord as an ending chord, it works beautifully.

The chord tones and tensions for CΔ7#5 are as follows:

Major 7#5 add 9 Chords

Major 7#5 add #11 Chords

Basic Intervals Answers

ANSWER PAGES

The following pages contain the answers to all the exercises presented in this book. Keep in mind that because the same note can appear in many different places on the guitar neck, there can be more than one correct answer to each exercise. If you would like a complete list of answers for each exercise you can download the alternative answers at www.muse-eek.com The answers found on the following pages and on the alternative answer pages on the muse-eek website limit the range to five frets on the guitar fretboard. Five frets in the most comfortable and practical range for most guitarist's hands. There are of course even more possible answers but they would use uncomfortably large stretches or totally unplayable combinations.

Muse Eek hosts a secure area of their website for customers who own their books. This secure area provides additional resources for the serious student. At this time there is no additional charge for this information; just register and receive a password to enter it. This secure section is an ongoing project provided by Muse Eek, containing extra help files, video clips, and other educational information.

Our goal at Muse Eek is to provide the best distance learning resource for music, and any suggestions to augment or improve the site are welcomed. Please e-mail us at info@muse-eek.com

Larger Intervals Answers

Major Triads Answers

Minor Triads Answers

Diminished Triads Answers

Augmented Triads Answers

Suspended 4th Triads Answers

Minor Seventh Chords Answers

Dominant Seventh Chords Answers

116

Dominant 7sus4 Chords Answers

Minor 7b5 Chords Answers

Diminished 7th Chords Answers

119

Minor Major 7th Chords Answers

Major 7#11 Chords Answers

Dominant 7b5 Chords Answers

123

Dominant 7#5 Chords Answers

Major Sixth Chords Answers

Minor Sixth Chords Answers

Major 7 9 Chords Answers

127

Major 7 6 Chords Answers

Major 7 6 #11 Chords Answers

Major 7 9 #11 Chords Answers

130

Major 7 6 9 Chords Answers

Major 6 9 Chords Answers

Major add 9 Chords Answers

134

Major 7 6 9 #11 Chords Answers

135

Minor 9 Chords Answers

Minor 911 Chords Answers

137

Minor 6 9 Chords Answers

Minor 6 9 11 Chords Answers

139

Minor 11 Chords Answers

Minor 6 11 Chords Answers

Minor 6 7 Chords Answers

Minor 7 6 9 Chords Answers

Dominant 9th Chords Answers

Dominant 7b9 Chords Answers

Dominant 7#9 Chords Answers

146

Dominant 13th Chords Answers

Dominant 7 b13 Chords Answers

Dominant 9 13th Chords Answers

Dominant 9 b13 Chords Answers

Dominant 13b9 Chords Answers

151

Dominant 13#9 Chords Answers

Dominant 7 b9 b13 Chords Answers

Dominant 7 #9 b13 Chords Answers

Dominant 9 #11 Chords Answers

Dominant 7 b9 #11 Chords Answers

156

Dominant 7 b13 #11 Chords Answers

Dominant 9sus4 Chords Answers

Dominant 7 sus4 b9 Chords Answers

Dominant 7sus4#9 Chords Answers

Dominant 13sus4 Chords Answers

Dominant 7 sus4 b13 Chords Answers

164

Dominant 9sus4 add 13 Chords Answers

Dominant 13sus4b9 Chords Answers

Dominant 13sus4#9 Chords Answers

Minor 7b5 add 9 Chords Answers

Minor 7b5 add b13 Chords Answers

Diminished 7th add 9 Chords Answers

Diminished 7th add 11 Chords Answers

Diminished 7th add b13 Chords Answers

176

Minor Major 79 Chords Answers

Minor Major 7 11 Chords Answers

Minor Major 7 6 Chords Answers

Minor Major 7 9 11 Chords Answers

Minor Major 7b5 Chords Answers

Minor Major 7b5 add 9 Chords Answers

Major 7#5 add 9 Chords Answers

Major 7#5 add #11 Chords Answers

Blank Answer Worksheet for Further Study

Books Available From
Muse Eek Publishing Company

The Bruce Arnold series of instruction books for guitar are the result of 20 years of teaching. Mr. Arnold, who teaches at New York University and Princeton University has listened to the questions and problems of his students, and written forty books addressing the needs of the beginning to advanced student. Written in a direct, friendly and practical manner, each book is structured in such as way as to enable a student to understand, retain and apply musical information. In short, these books teach.

Chord Workbook for Guitar Volume 1 (2nd edition)
ISBN 0-9648632-1-9

A consistent seller, this book addresses the needs of the beginning through intermediate student. The beginning student will learn chords on the guitar, and a section is also included to help learn the basics of music theory. Progressions are provided to help a student apply these chords to common sequences. The more advanced student will find the reharmonization section to be an invaluable resource of harmonic choices. Information is given through musical notation as well as tablature.

Chord Workbook for Guitar Volume 2 (2nd edition)
ISBN 0-9648632-3-5

This book is the Rosetta stone of pop/jazz chords, and is geared to the intermediate to advanced student. *These are the chords that any serious student bent on a musical career must know.* Unlike other books which simply give examples of isolated chords, this unique book provides a comprehensive series of progressions and chord combinations which are immediately applicable to both composition and performance.

Music Theory Workbook for Guitar Series

The world's most popular instrument, the guitar, is not taught in our public schools. In addition, it is one of the hardest on which to learn the basics of music. As a result, it is frequently difficult for the serious guitarist to get a firm foundation in theory.

Theory Workbook for Guitar Volume 1 ISBN 0-9648632-4-3
This book provides real hands-on application of intervals and chords. A theory section written in concise and easy to understand language prepares the student for all exercises. Worksheets are given that quiz a student about intervals and chord construction using staff notation and guitar tablature. Answers are supplied in the back of the book enabling a student to work without a teacher.

Theory Workbook for Guitar Volume 2 ISBN 0-9648632-5-1
This book provides real hands-on application for 22 different scale types. A theory section written in concise and easy to understand language prepares the student for all exercises. Worksheets are given that quiz a student about scale construction using staff notation and guitar tablature. Answers are supplied in the back of the book enabling a student to work without a teacher. Audio files are also available on the muse-eek.com website to facilitate practice and improvisation with all the scales presented.

Rhythm Book Series

These books are a breakthrough in music instruction, using the internet as a teaching tool! Audio files of all the exercises are easily downloaded from the internet.

Rhythm Primer ISBN 0-890944-03-3

This 61 page book concentrates on all basic rhythms using four rhythmic levels. All examples use one pitch, allowing the student to focus completely on time and rhythm. All exercises can be downloaded from the internet to facilitate learning. See http://www.muse-eek.com for details.

Rhythms Volume 1 ISBN 0-9648632-7-8

This 120 page book concentrates on eighth note rhythms and is a thesaurus of rhythmic patterns. All examples use one pitch, allowing the student to focus completely on time and rhythm. All exercises can be downloaded from the internet to facilitate learning. See http://www.muse-eek.com for details.

To order books:
from your local music store, bookstore use the ISBN number or
on-line at amazon.com and barnesandnoble.com
or direct from:

Muse Eek Publishing Company
P.O. Box 509
New York, New York 10276
phone: 212-473-7030   fax: 212-473-4601

Audio examples and more information can be found on the internet at www.muse-eek.com

Rhythms Volume 2 ISBN   0-9648632-8-6

This volume concentrates on sixteenth note rhythms, and is a 108 page thesaurus of rhythmic patterns. All examples use one pitch, allowing the student to focus completely on time and rhythm. All exercises can be downloaded from the internet to facilitate learning. See http://www.muse-eek.com for details.

Rhythms Volume 3 ISBN   0-890944-04-1

This volume concentrates on thirty second note rhythms, and is a 102 page thesaurus of rhythmic patterns. All examples use one pitch, allowing the student to focus completely on time and rhythm. All exercises can be downloaded from the internet to facilitate learning. See http://www.muse-eek.com for details.

Odd Meters Volume 1 ISBN 0-9648632-9-4

This book applies both eighth and sixteenth note rhythms to odd meter combinations. All examples use one pitch, allowing the student to focus completely on time and rhythm. Exercises can be downloaded from the internet to facilitate learning. This 100 page book is an essential sight reading tool.
See http://www.muse-eek.com for details.

Contemporary Rhythms Volume 1 ISBN 1-890944-27-0

This volume concentrates on eight note rhythms and is a thesaurus of rhythmic patterns. Each exercise uses one pitch which allows the student to focus completely on time and rhythm. Exercises use modern innovations common to twentieth century notation, thereby familiarizing the student with the most sophisticated systems likely to be encountered in the course of a musical career. All exercises can be downloaded from the internet to facilitate learning. See http://www.muse-eek.com for details.

Contemporary Rhythms Volume 2 ISBN 1-890944-28-9

This volume concentrates on sixteenth note rhythms and is a thesaurus of rhythmic patterns. Each exercise uses one pitch which allows the student to focus completely on time and rhythm. Exercise use modern innovations common to twentieth century notation, thereby familiarizing the student with the most sophisticated systems likely to be encountered in the course of a musical career. All exercises can be downloaded from the internet to facilitate learning. See http://www.muse-eek.com for details.

Independence Volume 1   ISBN 1-890944-00-9

This 51 page book is designed for pianists, stick and touchstyle guitarists, percussionists and anyone who wishes to develop the rhythmic independence of their hands. This volume concentrates on quarter, eighth and sixteenth note rhythms and is a thesaurus of rhythmic patterns. The exercises in this book gradually incorporate more and more complex rhythmic patterns making it an excellent tool for both the beginning and the advanced student.

Other Guitar Study Aids

Guitar Clinic
ISBN 1-890944-45-9

Guitar Clinic" contains techniques and exercises Mr. Arnold uses in the clinics and workshops he gives throughout the United States and is written as a response to the many questions students have asked him over the years. Essential information and instruction is given in clear, easy to understand language, addressing the needs of both beginning and advanced students. Topics covered include: how to read music, sight reading, reading rhythms, music theory, chord and scale construction, modal sequencing, approach notes, reharmonization, bass and chord comping, and hexatonic scales.

Right Hand Technique for Guitar Volume 1
ISBN 0-9648632-6-X

Here's a breakthrough in music instruction, using the internet as a teaching tool! This book gives a concise method for developing right hand technique on the guitar, one of the most overlooked and under-addressed aspects of learning the instrument. The simplest, most basic movements are used to build fatigue-free and virtuousic technique. Exercises can be downloaded from the internet to facilitate learning. See http://www.muse-eek.com for details.

To order books:
from your local music store, bookstore use the ISBN number or
on-line at amazon.com and barnesandnoble.com
or direct from:

Muse Eek Publishing Company
P.O. Box 509
New York, New York 10276
phone: 212-473-7030   fax: 212-473-4601

Audio examples and more information can be found on the internet at www.muse-eek.com

Single String Studies Volume One ISBN 1-890944-01-7

This book is an excellent learning tool for both the beginner who has no experience reading music on the guitar, and the advanced student looking to improve their ledger line reading and general knowledge of each string of the guitar. Each exercise concentrates a students attention of one string at a time. This allows a familiarity to form between the written pitch and where it can be found on the guitar along with improving one's "feel" for jumping linearly across the guitar neck. Exercises can be downloaded from the internet to facilitate learning. See http://www.muse-eek.com for details.

Single String Studies Volume Two ISBN 1-890944-05-X

This book is a continuation of volume one but now using non-diatonic notes. Volume two helps the intermediate and advanced student improve their ledger line reading and general knowledge of each string of the guitar. Each exercise concentrates a students attention of one string at a time. This allows a familiarity to form between the written pitch and where it can be found on the guitar along with improving one's "feel" for jumping linearly across the guitar neck. Exercises can be downloaded from the internet to facilitate learning. See http://www.muse-eek.com for details.

Single String Studies Volume One (Bass Clef) ISBN 1-890944-02-5

This book is an excellent learning tool for both the beginner who has no experience reading music on the bass guitar, and the advanced student looking to improve their ledger line reading and general knowledge of each string of the bass. Each exercise concentrates a students attention of one string at a time. This allows a familiarity to form between the written pitch and where it can be found on the bass along with improving one's "feel" for jumping linearly across the fretboard. Exercises can be downloaded from the internet to facilitate learning. See http://www.muse-eek.com for details.

Single String Studies Volume Two (Bass Clef) ISBN 1-890944-06-8

This book is a continuation of volume one but now using non-diatonic notes. Volume two helps the intermediate and advanced student improve their ledger line reading and general knowledge of each string of the bass. Each exercise concentrates a students attention of one string at a time. This allows a familiarity to form between the written pitch and where it can be found on the bass along with improving one's "feel" for jumping linearly across the fretboard.

Sight Singing and Ear Training Series

The world is full of ear training and sight reading books, so why do we need more? This sight singing and ear training series uses a different method of teaching relative pitch sight singing and ear training. The success of this method has been astounding. Along with a new method of ear training these books also use CDs and the internet as a teaching tool! Audio files of all the exercises are easily downloaded from the internet at www.muse-eek.com By combining interactive audio files with a new approach to ear training a student's progress is limited only by their willingness to practice!

A Fanatic's Guide to Ear Training and Sight Singing
ISBN 1-890944-19-X

This book and CD present a method for developing good pitch recognition through sight singing. This method differs from the myriad of other sight singing books in that it develops the ability to identify and name all twelve pitches within a key center. Through this method a student gains the ability to identify sound based on it's relationship to a key and not the relationship of one note to another i.e. interval training as commonly taught in many texts. All note groupings from one to six notes are presented giving the student a thesaurus of basic note combinations which develops sight singing and note recognition to a level unattainable before this Guide's existence.

Key Center Recognition ISBN 1-890944-30-3

This book and CD present a method for developing the ability to recognize the function of any note against a key. This method is a must for anyone who wishes to sound one note on an instrument or voice and instantly know what key a song is in. Through this method a student gains the ability to identify a sound based on its relationship to a key and not the relationship of one note to another i.e. interval training as commonly taught in many texts. Key Center Recognition is a definite requirement before proceeding to two note ear training.

LINES Volume One: Sight Reading and Sight Singing Exercises
ISBN 1-890944-09-2

This book can be used for many applications. It is an excellent source for easy half note melodies that a beginner can use to learn how to read music or for sight singing slightly chromatic lines. An intermediate or advanced student will find exercises for multi-voice reading. These exercises can also be used for multi-voice ear training. The book has the added benefit in that all exercises can be heard by downloading the audio files for each example. See http://www.muse-eek.com for details.

To order books:
from your local music store, bookstore use the ISBN number or
on-line at amazon.com and barnesandnoble.com
or direct from:

Muse Eek Publishing Company
P.O. Box 509
New York, New York 10276
phone: 212-473-7030   fax: 212-473-4601

Audio examples and more information can be found on the internet at www.muse-eek.com

Ear Training ONE NOTE: Beginning Level ISBN 1-890944-12-2

This Book and Audio CD presents a new and exciting method of developing relative pitch ear training. It has been used with great success and is now finally available on CD.   There are three levels available depending on the student's ability. There are three levels available depending on the student's ability.   This beginning level is recommended for students who have little or no music training.

Ear Training ONE NOTE: Intermediate Level   ISBN 1-890944-13-0

This Audio CD and booklet presents a new and exciting method of developing relative pitch ear training. It has been used with great success and is now finally available on CD. This intermediate level is recommended for students who have had some music training but still find their skills need more development.

Ear Training ONE NOTE: Advanced Level   ISBN 1-890944-14-9

This Audio CD and booklet presents a new and exciting method of developing relative pitch ear training. It has been used with great success and is now finally available on CD.   There are three levels available depending on the student's ability.   This advanced level is recommended for students who have worked with the intermediate level and now wish to perfect their skills.

Ear Training TWO NOTE: Beginning Level Volume One
ISBN 1-890944-31-9

This Book and Audio CD continues the new and exciting method of developing relative pitch ear training as set forth in the "Ear Training, One Note" series.   There are six volume in the beginning level series. Through practice, the student eventually gains the ability to recognize the key and the names of any two notes played simultaneously. Volume One concentrates on 5ths. Prerequisite: a strong grasp of the One Note method.

Ear Training TWO NOTE: Beginning Level Volume Two
ISBN 1-890944-32-7

This Book and Audio CD continues the new and exciting method of developing relative pitch ear training as set forth in the "Ear Training, One Note" series. There are six volume in the beginning level series. Through practice, the student eventually gains the ability to recognize the key and the names of any two notes played simultaneously. Volume Two concentrates on 3rds. Prerequisite: a strong grasp of the One Note method.

Ear Training TWO NOTE: Beginning Level Volume Three
ISBN 1-890944-33-5

This Book and Audio CD continues the new and exciting method of developing relative pitch ear training as set forth in the "Ear Training, One Note" series. There are six volume in the beginning level series. Through practice, the student eventually gains the ability to recognize the key and the names of any two notes played simultaneously. Volume Three concentrates on 6ths. Prerequisite: a strong grasp of the One Note method.

Ear Training TWO NOTE: Beginning Level Volume Four
ISBN 1-890944-34-3

This Book and Audio CD continues the new and exciting method of developing relative pitch ear training as set forth in the "Ear Training, One Note" series. There are six volume in the beginning level series. Through practice, the student eventually gains the ability to recognize the key and the names of any two notes played simultaneously. Volume Four concentrates on 4ths. Prerequisite: a strong grasp of the One Note method.

Ear Training TWO NOTE: Beginning Level Volume Five
ISBN 1-890944-35-1

This Book and Audio CD continues the new and exciting method of developing relative pitch ear training as set forth in the "Ear Training, One Note" series. There are six volume in the beginning level series. Through practice, the student eventually gains the ability to recognize the key and the names of any two notes played simultaneously. Volume Five concentrates on 2nds. Prerequisite: a strong grasp of the One Note method.

Ear Training TWO NOTE: Beginning Level Volume Six
ISBN 1-890944-36-X

This Book and Audio CD continues the new and exciting method of developing relative pitch ear training as set forth in the "Ear Training, One Note" series. There are six volume in the beginning level series. Through practice, the student eventually gains the ability to recognize the key and the names of any two notes played simultaneously. Volume Six concentrates on 7ths. Prerequisite: a strong grasp of the One Note method.

To order books:
from your local music store, bookstore use the ISBN number or
on-line at amazon.com and barnesandnoble.com
or direct from:

Muse Eek Publishing Company
P.O. Box 509
New York, New York 10276
phone: 212-473-7030   fax: 212-473-4601

Audio examples and more information can be found on the internet at www.muse-eek.com

Comping Styles Series

This series builds off from the progressions found in Chord Workbook Volume One. Each book covers a specific style of music and presents exercises to help a guitarist, bassist or drummer master that style. Audio CDs are also available so a student can play along with each example and really get "into the groove".

Comping Styles for the Guitar Volume Two FUNK
ISBN 1-890944-07-6

This volume teaches a student how to play guitar or piano in a funk style. 36 Progressions are presented: 12 keys of a Major and Minor Blues plus 12 keys of Rhythm Changes A different groove is presented for each exercise giving the student a wide range of funk rhythms to master.   An Audio CD is also included so a student can play along with each example and really get "into the groove". The audio CD contains "trio" versions of each exercise with Guitar, Bass and Drums.

Comping Styles for the Bass Volume Two FUNK
ISBN 1-890944-08-4

This volume teaches a student how to play bass in a funk style. 36 Progressions are presented: 12 keys of a Major and Minor Blues plus 12 keys of Rhythm Changes A different groove is presented for each exercise giving the student a wide range of funk rhythms to master.   An Audio CD is also included so a student can play along with each example and really get "into the groove". The audio CD contains "trio" versions of each exercise with Guitar, Bass and Drums.

Time Series

The Doing Time series presents a method for gaining control of your internal time sense: This series is an excellent source for any musician who is serious about developing strong internal sense of time. This is particularly useful in any kind of music where the rhythms and time signatures may be very complex or free, and there is no conductor.

THE BIG METRONOME
ISBN   1-890944-37-8

The Big Metronome is designed to help you develop a better internal sense of time. This is accomplished by requiring you to "feel time" rather than having you rely on the steady click of a metronome. The idea is to slowly wean yourself away from an external device and rely on your internal/natural sense of time. The exercises presented work in conjunction with the three CDs that accompany this book. CD 1 presents the first 13 settings from a traditional metronome 40-66; the second CD contains metronome markings 69-116, and the third CD contains metronome markings 120-208. The first CD gives you a 2 bar count off and a click every measure, the second CD gives you a 2 bar count off and a click every 2 measures, the 3rd CD gives you a 2 bar count off and a click every 4 measures. By presenting all common metronome markings a student can use these 3 CDs as a replacement for a traditional metronome.

Doing Time with the Blues Volume One:
ISBN 1-890944-17-3

The book and CD presents a method for gaining an internal sense of time thereby eliminating dependence on a metronome.. The book presents the basic concept for developing good time and also includes exercises that can be practiced with the CD. The CD provides eight 8 minute tracks at different tempos in which the time is delineated every 2 bars, and with an extra hit every 12 bars to outline the blues form. The student may then use the exercises presented in the book to gain control of their execution or improvise to gain control of their ideas using this bare minimum of time delineation.

Doing Time with the Blues Volume Two:
ISBN 1-890944-18-1

This is the 2nd volume of a four volume series which presents a method for developing a musician's internal sense of time, thereby eliminating dependence on a metronome.. This 2nd volume presents different exercises which further the development of this time sense. This 2nd volume begins to test even a professional level player's ability. The CD provides eight 8 minute tracks at different tempos in which the time is delineated every 4 bars with an extra hit every 12 bars to outline the blues form.   New exercises are also included that can be practiced with the CD. This series is an excellent source for any musician who is serious about developing an internal sense of time.

Doing Time with the Blues Volume Three:
ISBN 1-890944-20-3

This is the 3rd volume of a four volume series which presents a method for developing a musician's internal sense of time, thereby eliminating dependence on a metronome. This 3rd volume presents different exercises which further the development of this sense of time, and will give even professional players a run for their money. The CD provides eight 8 minute tracks at different

To order books:
from your local music store, bookstore use the ISBN number or
on-line at amazon.com and barnesandnoble.com
or direct from:

Muse Eek Publishing Company
P.O. Box 509
New York, New York 10276
phone: 212-473-7030   fax: 212-473-4601

Audio examples and more information can be found on the internet at www.muse-eek.com

tempos in which the time is delineated every 6 bars with an extra hit every 12 bars to outline the blues form. The combination of specific exercises to be played in conjunction with the CD makes for a very challenging workout. This series is an excellent source for any musician who is serious about developing their internal sense of time.

Doing Time with the Blues Volume Four:
ISBN 1-890944-21-1

This is the culmination of a four volume series which presents a method for developing a musician's internal sense of time, thereby eliminating dependence on a metronome. This 4th volume presents more complex exercises and drills for developing an internal sense of time, and will challenge the most demanding professional level musician. The CD provides eight 8 minute tracks at different tempos in which the time is delineated every 12 bars outlining the blues form. The combination of advanced exercises to be played in time with the long silences on the CD makes for a very challenging workout. This series is an excellent source for any musician who is serious about developing their internal sense of time.

Doing Time with 32 bars Volume One:
ISBN 1-890944-22-X

The book and CD presents a method for gaining an internal sense of time thereby eliminating dependence on a metronome. The book presents the basic concept for developing good time and also includes exercises that can be practiced with the CD. The CD provides eight 8 minute tracks at different tempos in which the time is delineated every 2 bars, with an extra hit every 32 to outline the 32 bar form. The student may then use the exercises presented in the book to gain control of their execution or improvise to gain control of their ideas using this bare minimum of time delineation.

Doing Time with 32 bars Volume Two:
ISBN 1-890944-23-8

This is the 2nd volume of a four volume series which presents a method for developing a musician's internal sense of time, thereby eliminating dependence on a metronome.. This 2nd volume presents different exercises which further the development of this time sense. This 2nd volume begins to test even a professional level player's ability. The CD provides eight 8 minute tracks at different tempos in which the time is delineated every 4 bars with an extra hit every 32 bars to outline the 32 bar form. New exercises are also included that can be practiced with the CD. This series is an excellent source for any musician who is serious about developing an internal sense of time.

Doing Time with 32 bars Volume Three:
ISBN 1-890944-24-6

This is the 3rd volume of a four volume series which presents a method for developing a musician's internal sense of time, thereby eliminating dependence on a metronome. This 3rd volume presents different exercises which further the development of this sense of time, and will give even professional players a run for their money. The CD provides eight 8 minute tracks at different tempos in which the time is delineated every 8 bars with an extra hit every 32 bars to outline the 32 bar form. The combination of specific exercises to be played in conjunction with the CD makes for a very challenging workout. This series is an excellent source for any musician who is serious about developing their internal sense of time.

Doing Time with 32 bars Volume Four:
ISBN 1-890944-25-4

This is the fourth volume in this series which presents a method for developing a musician's internal sense of time, thereby eliminating dependence on a metronome. This 4th volume presents more complex exercises and drills for developing an internal sense of time, and will challenge the most demanding professional level musician. The CD provides eight 8 minute tracks at different tempos in which the time is delineated every 16 bars with an extra hit every 32 to outline the 32 bar form. The combination of advanced exercises to be played in time with the long silences on the CD makes for a very challenging workout. This series is an excellent source for any musician who is serious about developing their internal sense of time.

Doing Time with 32 bars Volume Five:
ISBN 1-890944-26-2

This is the culmination of a five volume series which presents a method for developing a musician's internal sense of time, thereby eliminating dependence on a metronome. This 5th volume presents different exercises which further the development of a strong internal sense of time. The CD gives you eight 8 minute tracks at different tempos in which the time is delineated every 32 bars. When you have mastered this one, you can throw your wristwatch away! This series is an excellent source for any musician who is serious about developing their internal sense of time.

To order books:
from your local music store, bookstore use the ISBN number or
on-line at amazon.com and barnesandnoble.com
or direct from:

Muse Eek Publishing Company
P.O. Box 509
New York, New York 10276
phone: 212-473-7030   fax: 212-473-4601

Audio examples and more information can be found on the internet at www.muse-eek.com

Bruce Arnold's critically acclaimed CD "A Few Dozen" is now available directly through Muse—Eek Publishing at a great price!

Reviews of "A Few Dozen:"

"Arnold's music--as performed by his trio, with drummer Tony Moreno and bassist Ratzo B. Harris-- never loses its contact with jazz, even when both the linear and clustered sounds emerge in unexpectedly acerbic fashion....he deserves credit for his effort to expand the potential of the jazz palette."

---Don Heckman, The Los Angeles Times

"Arnold does an exceptional job of taking that scale which is usually emplyed by avant-garde and classical musicians and slipping it into the jazz form"

James Lien, CMJ New Music Report

"There's a gentility to the guitarist's work even when it gets ready to rum - ble. That makes the new trio outing "A Few Dozen" both lyrical and jagged."

Jim Macnie, The Village Voice

"This is complex, heady adventurous, open-ended music fronted by Arnold's resonant, slightly steely, dusty, distant, single note sound that straddles the line between jazz tradition and rock snarling. There's a healthy cynicism that pervades Arnold's music making it all his own."

Michael Nastos, The All Music Guide

To get your copy of "A Few Dozen" for just $10.00 (this includes shipping!) simply send us a Xerox copy of the cover of this book along with the order form on the next page.

Check out www.muse-eek.com for a complete listing of available books, CDs, and special discounts

I WOULD LIKE TO ORDER THE FOLLOWING BOOKS/CDs:

Please enclose your check or money order, payable to Muse-eek Publishing Company. For Visa, MasterCard or AMEX please include your card information below.

Quantity   Author/Title   ISBN # if book   Price

_____ _____ _____ _____

_____ _____ _____ _____

_____ _____ _____ _____

_____ _____ _____ _____

_____ _____ _____ _____

_____ _____ _____ _____

_____ _____ _____

* No postage or handling for orders within the U.S.A.
INTERNATIONAL SHIPPING CHARGES
$6.00 for the first book ordered
$3.50 for each additional book.
$3.00 for each CD.

                                      Subtotal   _____

                       *Postage and Handling   _____

                                TOTAL   _____

[   ] I have enclosed a personal check or money order.

[   ] I would like to charge my order to : [   ] MasterCard   [   ] Visa   [   ] AMEX

Card Number   Ship to:

_____   _____

Expiration

_____   _____

Signature

_____   _____

Daytime Phone

_____

Allow 1 week for delivery for U.S. orders. Allow 2 weeks for International Orders.

Return this order form to:

Muse-eek Publishing Company, P.O. Box 509 New York N.Y. 10276